Missing Persons

Kirsty Adlard

Published by

Dayglo Books Ltd, Nottingham, UK

www.dayglobooks.co.uk

Cover artwork & illustrations by
www.valentineart.co.uk

Typeset in Opendyslexic
byAbelardo Gonzales (2013)

Printed by IngramSpark

Distributed by Filament Publishing Ltd, Croydon

Missing Persons

CHAPTER 1

It's great when my birthday falls on a Saturday.
No school to prepare for and Mum always clears space
on the breakfast table and piles up my cards and
presents.

I reach for my hot chocolate, then start to slice
open the envelopes. There's always a present and
a card from my old friend, Isabel.

As I read her card today, memories of my
birthday seven years ago come flooding back so clearly.
How could I ever forget?

It is the 9th of September 1943. My ninth birthday. The 9th day of the 9th month and I'm 9.

999 means nothing to me. I don't associate it with emergencies. But this day certainly proves to be a day of emergencies.

I've been allowed to invite my best friend from school, Isabel. We shall share a picnic including windfall apples, plums and pears from our orchard.   She'll take some fruit home to her Mum to stew and enjoy, if she wants.

I am hovering by the kitchen doorway, far too early, watching for Isabel's bicycle to appear on the rough path across the fields to our house.

Instead, a bright red Post Office cycle approaches the door and Willie, the post-mistress's son dismounts and breathlessly asks for Mum.

Daddy volunteered for army service in the Royal Engineers as soon as war broke out, despite my mother's pleas.

For the first three years he served in Great Britain, but I knew, from the letters he sent me, that he left for service abroad after his leave six months ago. That was the last time we saw him.

Mum's normally ruddy face turns pale at the sight of the orange envelope which Willie hands her.

"Sorry, Mrs Morris, I doubt if this will contain good news." His grubby face looks almost as glum as my Mum's.

Ours is a close-knit community, even though we only joined it at the outbreak of war.

Mum sits down on the chipped, cream-painted kitchen chair by the back door, in the sunshine. Her trembling fingers hold the envelope as she clumsily

slides her thumb beneath the flap.

"No, there's no reply, Willie. Thanks."

I know that Willie's pocket money consists of

small tips given him in appreciation of his cycle rides in

the heat, but no such thought crosses Mum's mind as

she turns her tear-stained face towards me.

"Sorry, love, you'll have to go to Isabel's and put

her off coming. I can't cope with birthday celebrations

after this news – it's Daddy, of course. Missing,

believed dead."

She pulls me towards her. Not normally

a demonstrative mother, her hug says it all.

CHAPTER 2

When I return from Isabel's house, where I cancelled my party invitation, there is no sign of Mum in the kitchen.

I hear a weak cry from upstairs.

Is Mum suffering shock at the news of Daddy's possible death? She is very thin and poorly, so perhaps it's a difficult pregnancy at 42 years of age. Is it putting too much strain on her? I don't know.

I dash upstairs and find Mum in bed. I get no greeting, just an urgent message to deliver.

"Sorry to be a nuisance, love," Mum whispers. "You'll have to get on your bike again and ride to Mrs Buchan's. Tell her Mrs Morris has started labour and feels it'll be a quick birth. Can you remember that? She needs to come right away, tell her."

I feel my knees start to tremble as Mum's face puckers in pain. I've never seen her like this before. I race downstairs, jump on my bike and pedal like the wind.

Mrs Buchan brings me home in the car with her. She says I can collect my bike any time, which is kind of her.

"Boil as much water as you can, there's a good girl," she instructs. "But be very careful – don't try to carry the kettles when the water's boiling. I'll be back to do that as soon as I've popped up to see your Mum. Where do you keep clean towels? But your mother's a sensible woman. She'll have prepared everything, I'm sure."

With that, she stomps up the stairs and I start to fill kettles and pans as she's told me. I only get as far as the big kettle when I can hear the midwife's loud exclamation from above.

"Oh, my God," she shouts, "you said it'd be a quick birth, but I didn't anticipate it would be that quick!"

I race up the stairs, determined to be the first family member to be in on this exciting event. But my enthusiasm quickly turns to concern when Mrs. Buchan firmly closes the bedroom door.

"Not just yet, my dear. Just let me make your mum comfy. I'll call when she's ready."

Then she adds: "But I can tell you that you have a new little brother."

I don't know whether to be pleased or sorry at this news. I had secretly hoped our new baby would be a girl.

Isabel and I would be able to dress her in pretty clothes and push her about in my big old dolls' pram. That would be much more fun than the dolls I'd had passed down from an older cousin.

All of these poor things were tossed aside in my toy box. When I asked if we could take them to the dolls' hospital in the nearby town, Mum said their broken heads would be too costly to replace.

"Right you are, Marion, you can come and see your brother now."

I scurry up the stairs as fast as I can.

At least he's an unexpected birthday present, I tell myself, even if I'd rather have had a sister. I push open the bedroom door cautiously.

I've never seen a new born baby and I don't want to frighten it.

Me frighten him? More like the other way round. I clench my nails in the palms of my hands to stop myself crying out in horror. A more red, screwed up, cross looking face I've never seen.

I avoid Mum's enquiring look as she waits for my delighted reaction.

CHAPTER 3

"So, what d'you think of him, love? Isn't he the best birthday present you could ever have?" the midwife simpers encouragingly.

"Yes, he's nice, Mrs Buchan," I try to inject some enthusiasm into my voice, but I can tell I've barely succeeded.

My English teacher at school says that people use 'nice' when they've got nothing better to say. But that is still the most enthusiastic word I can come up with.

"You okay, Mum?" I am concerned at my mother's weary face. Although she holds the baby lovingly, she seems just too drained by her recent experience to do anything but nod – despite ithaving been such a quick birth.

"She'll be fine after a good night's sleep," Mrs Buchan answers for Mum. "Now, is there enough boiling water to make us all a nice strong cup of tea?"

I nod silently, then tell them both – "We can all have a piece of the Victoria sandwich cake Mum made for my birthday, if you like."

Mrs Buchan smiles as she tidies the bedroom, sorting the bloodied sheets and towels into bundles, ready to soak in salty water, then go in the old brick copper next day, to be boiled.

She's seen this so many times before, I suppose, but she still seems to have that aura of

pride, as if she really believes that most of the hard
work to produce this child has been done by her.

Mrs Buchan called each day for a fortnight after
the birth. She was concerned that the responsibilities of
post-natal care might be more than a nine-year-old
could adequately cope with.

"So your brother's going to be called Hugh, after
your Daddy, your mother tells me," she comments
conversationally, over the daily hot drink
I manage to make for us all, from a bottle of coffee
essence.

"Your Mum's going on fine now, you know.
I think you could go back to school next week. It
doesn't do to miss too much schooling at your age.
Your Mum's getting up a little longer each day now and
Hugh seems to be thriving, don't you think?"

Mrs Buchan becomes quite a friend to me during

this difficult period. She seems to treat me as almost an equal, yet she carefully supervises any adult tasks I need to undertake.

Each day she checks that Mum and I have planned a menu for the rest of the day.

She helps Mum to register Hugh's birth and helps with the necessary paperwork from the army. Mum's 'separation allowance' is converted to a small 'widow's pension'.

The money takes into account the third, and most important, mouth to feed.

CHAPTER 4

"I've told your Mum you'll not be here for an hour
or so," Mrs Buchan volunteered.

"You can have a lift with me to come and collect
your bike and do a bit of shopping to bring back, to last
you over the weekend.

"On Monday, when you're back at school,
I'll make one final visit and bring your Mum some eggs.
She'll be able to scramble or fry those with a rasher of
bacon for mid-day and you'll have had your school
dinner, so you should both be fine."

Gradually, Mum regained her strength and our lives returned to something approaching the routine we'd followed prior to Daddy's death.

It had now been confirmed by an official letter that Daddy was killed while erecting a temporary bridge for the troops to cross a stream which had swollen into a rushing river after a storm.

Mum had not regained her previous energy and zest for life. Everybody from the vicar down to serious-faced little Willie from the Post Office kept telling us: 'it's early days yet,' and we tried to keep this foremost in our minds and believe that things would get better.

I'll never forget that miserable dreary time. I don't know who I was most sorry for – Mum or myself. We both missed Daddy so much. And Hugh, of course, would never know him. Money, or the lack of it, was anotheroverwhelming worry.

At Christmas time, the glass-fronted notice board in the Post Office suddenly overflowed with little hand-written appeals. Some were for out-grown toys and clothing, or bicycles of various sizes.

Others were for part-time staff, both in the Post Office itself, or in local village shops.

The two village pubs had manage to remain stocked up through the war years and they were advertising for help too.

The landlord of the Rose and Crown, Bert Pickering, had gone to the village school with Daddy. He had been particularly upset at the news of Daddy's death.

CHAPTER 5

One gloomy December Saturday, I heard
a knock on the back door. I opened it and found Mr
Pickering outside. He removed his cycle clips and shook
a frosting of snow from his checked cap.

He looked into Hugh's pram, and received
a toothless grin from the baby in return. Then with
raised eyebrows he queried:

"Your Mum at home, Marion? Or have I called at
the wrong time?"

I shouted up the stairs to where Mum was
giving the bedrooms a good clean. She came down to

the kitchen, frantically trying to tidy her hair
and remove her apron.

"Why, it's you, Bert! The last person
I expected to see – we don't have many visitors here,
especially in the winter, as you can imagine. Have you
time for a cuppa? You look frozen!"

Without waiting for an answer, she pulled the
smoke-blackened old kettle over the flames and
reached for the teapot and mugs for us all.

"That's very kind of you, Sylvia. That's the best
invitation I've had all afternoon!"

Mr Pickering held his hands towards the fire,
rubbing them together. Then he blew his nose.

"What it is, you see . . . I know you must be
finding it difficult to make ends meet and . . .
I thought . . . as I need extra evening bar staff

over Christmas, I wondered if we could come to some arrangement?"

He pulled the steaming mug of tea towards him and looked hopefully at Mum.

"Oh, but I couldn't, Bert! Not this soon, anyway. I'm still feeding this little fella, you see. And Marion's not old enough to take on the responsibility for the baby at her age, is she?"

Mum's regretful face was painful to see. She could certainly do with the money, as we all knew full well.

I wished it was my fourteenth birthday I'd celebrated in the summer, rather than my ninth.

"Give us until Easter, Bert, then I'll think about it again. I might feel more able to face folks by then. Marion will be that much older and the evenings will be lighter, too.

"It's ever so kind of you to think of me. I do appreciate it, really I do, but not just now . . . eh?"

"Yes. I suppose it was a fool's errand really, Sylv. I've certainly plenty of others who would be only too pleased to work an hour or two.

"But I just thought I'd like to offer it to you first, in your present situation . . . see what I mean?"

He drained the dregs of his tea, reached for his cap which had been drying near the fire, and pulled on his gloves and cycle clips.

"Happy Christmas, anyway," he exclaimed. "I know you're not a regular customer, so I may not see you again before then.

"Look after them both!" he smilingly told me. "I'll get back to open up before it gets too dark along your farm track. I don't know how you manage, tucked away down here."

Mum topped up our mugs again. We were both subdued. We were reluctant to admit to each other that we would have liked Mum to be able to take up Mr Pickering's offer of work.

But we both realised that it was just not possible while Hugh was so small.

CHAPTER 6

We knew that eventually Mum would need to look for a part-time evening job to eke out our finances.

As the weeks and months passed by I came to realise I had misjudged my baby brother.

His red face and wrinkles became smooth and soft, delightful to touch. Once his eyes began to focus, he responded to my cuddles and tickles. I loved him more than I could have possibly imagined at first.

Mum's face remained sad, and I often caught her day-dreaming in a world of her own.

But she also found satisfaction and pleasure in seeing Hugh and myself together – her 'little cubs' as she liked to call us.

It was a low-key Christmas in most households that year and particularly in our own. I managed to knit Hugh a little pair of mittens.

I unpicked the wool from a much-washed pink jumper I'd grown out of. With what was left I made a head-band to hold Mum's hair in place.

By saving up our sweet coupons for the month of December, Mum treated us all to chocolates. There were chocolate buttons for Hugh.

He dribbled more down his bib than he actually swallowed from his toothless mouth.

Mum and I had mint chocolates – our favourites.

Amongst the few Christmas cards we received

was a letter in an official-looking buff envelope. Mum was worried to death by it.

In fact, the letter helped us to solve the situation regarding part-time evening work.

The letter said we had to take in two teenage girls from the East End of London.

They were evacuees, being sent away from the city because of the danger from bombing raids.

Mum would be paid an allowance for having them.

The girls were sisters, named Frances and Freda Cook. They were to stay with us for as long as the war lasted.

Mum was instructed to fill in a form that came with the letter, and send it back. An inspection of our home would follow shortly.

CHAPTER 7

Both Mum and I scurried round the house, dusting and polishing. We made up twin beds in the spare bedroom.

We sorted through cupboards to see if there might be a prettier pair of curtains. Lined curtains would be best, because they would help keep out the cold.

We were already referring to 'the big girls' room', though the inspection had not yet taken place.

The fateful day arrived and a lady in uniform

from the Women's Voluntary Service knocked at the door. She walked around and then pronounced our house 'the cleanest home she'd seen for a long time.'

Mum asked some questions about the sisters. The lady assured us there would be no problem with head lice, as Frances and Freda, had been carefully examined and were clear.

It seemed most of the local residents preferred to take in boys. Any teenagers amongst them might prove useful, working in gardens or on a farm. In any case, boys were thought less of a worry and responsibility.

Even Hugh was enthusiastic, following the flurry of Frances and Freda's arrival. He thrust his little arms from side to side, like a conductor without his baton. He gave them his famous gummy grin, in response to their tummy tickles.

In no time, the girls spread all their clothes and shoes around their room, soon cancelling out our efforts to make it clean and tidy.

"Well, their heads may be clean, but I'm blowed if their faces are!" was Mum's comment as the girls slammed out of the back door.

"All that muck – lipstick and stuff, all over them. Never thought they'd be plastered up like that, when we were told they were twelve and thirteen."

To give them their due, the girls had asked Mum and me, quite politely, if they could borrow our bikes to pop down to the Post Office.

They wanted to send a card to their motherto let her know they had arrived safely.

"If they'd any sense, they'd have posted that before they left the village," Mum sniffed.

"Well, perhaps they hadn't been warned we live such a long way out," I defended them. "I hope they won't get my tyres punctured, else I'll be stuck for school on Monday."

Gradually, the girls settled in. It was a totally different life to the one they'd been used to, of course.

Now that Mum was almost back to normal physically, she tried to spend more and more time in the garden.

In the evenings, when I'd finished my home-work, Mum and I would thumb through seed catalogues and draw up plans of the garden, with numerous notes as to what would be sown in each area and when.

Although we had not discussed the matter in detail, I think there was an unspoken agreement between us that the female family members would gradually become vegetarian. Any meat or fish became a priority for Hugh, when he was weaned in the spring.

The 'East End' girls showed no inclination to help Mum and me in the garden, even when we explained to them that most of our food was home-produced and that without it, we would go hungry.

"We don't like any veggies, except peas," they retorted. "And there's always bread and jam, isn't there – that's what we have at home!"

CHAPTER 8

"Don't forget, sugar's rationed!" Mum snapped, when the girls demanded more bread and jam.

"Once this jam is finished I'll only be able to make very little. We've both given up sugar in our tea already! But runner beans – I can grow rows of them from seed I've saved."

With that, Mum returned to preparing vegetables for those who had the sense to eat them.

It soon became clear that the girls needed more social life than was usual in the country, and this caused

Mum concern. Now that she could push Hugh into the village, she discussed this with other women she met who were hosting girls. It seemed this was their experience too.

So when Bert Pickering again raised the question of part-time employment behind his bar, Mum felt it was time to strike a bargain with Frances and Freda.

"You two don't seem to mind which evening of the week you go out, do you?" she challenged the girls.

Reluctant nods of agreement – the girls obviously wondering what was to follow.

"Well, how would it be if you go out any weekday evening and then you stay here at home and keep an eye on Marion and Hugh at weekends? That's when the pub's extra busy and I'd be most help to Mr Pickering."

"Can we think about it a bit?" the girls

replied. "We don't know how our mates would feel about that, you see?"

They retired to their bedroom and there followed a whispered discussion. A few minutes later Frances called down the stairs:

"Would there be any payment for this baby-sitting, Auntie Sylvia? It's a big responsibility isn't it?"

"Payment? I should think not, indeed! It's to earn a bit of extra money I'd be going out myself," Mum hollered back. "You must have some home-work to do sometimes. Can't you do that on weekend evenings?"

With that, Mum slammed the kettle on the range.

Then she started making vegetable soup – for those of us who could stomach it, which included Hugh.

Luckily, she still had plenty of plum jam left on the shelf for these choosy girls to dig into.

A few days later the girls gloomily agreed that yes, they could curtail their social life. That would free up Mum to accept Mr Pickering's offer of weekend evening work.

She started the week before Easter, so that she could familiarise herself with her duties before what Bert hoped would be a busy weekend.

CHAPTER 9

All went well, apart from Mum feeling totally

exhausted by Sunday evenings.

We all benefited from her earnings, especially as

Hugh was out-growing his baby clothes so rapidly.

I was growing, too, and needed new school uniform.

Throughout the summer Mum was happy to cycle

to the Rose and Crown and pedal wearily back again at

around 11pm. She was ready to fall into bed with barely

the energy to wash her face.

She continued to work on our vegetable plot.

Until the weather turned really cold, baby Hugh could go outside with mum in the garden. He was well wrapped up in various pieces of thread-bare blanket and tucked in his pram.

I helped. We gathered and stored as many cooking and eating apples as we could.

A kindly neighbour climbed up Daddy's old ladder to reach the highest branches for us.

We bottled other fruits too – pears and plums. They were put away in the dark old pantry under the stairs.

We also had a few walnuts from our tree and hazelnuts I'd gathered from the hedgerows.

As the evenings began to shorten, Mum made sure the batteries in her cycle lamp were charged when she rode off to work. She wished the pub's closing time was not so late.

Although a country girl born and bred, she had always been nervous of the dark. She tried to avoid being out alone once daylight had faded.

One particular Sunday night I had a heavy cold. Although it was late, I couldn't get off to sleep.

I heard the back door open and crash shut, rather than being closed quietly. I could hear voices and muffled giggles downstairs.

I recognised Mum's whispers immediately, but there was a man's voice too. A few minutes later I heard the door opening. Almost immediately, it quietly closed again.

Should I go downstairs and check all was well with Mum? Or should I just wait to receive her nightly peek into my bedroom, before hearing her patter across the landing to her own room?

I decided to lie low and pretend to be asleep.

CHAPTER 10

Next morning, getting ready for school and feeding Hugh took everyone's attention.

No mention was made of any companion, male or female, bringing Mum home last night.

I turned the matter over in my mind all day. Before tea, I casually asked Mum if work had gone well last evening.

She seemed a little flustered at first. Then, as she stood at the sink with her back to me, peeling potatoes, she threw her reply over her shoulder.

"Yes. That fellow Nick was there again. I've told you about him before, I think? Last night heoffered to walk me home. Nice of him, wasn't it?"

She turned and eyed me self-consciously, trying to judge my reaction.

"Well, yes, I suppose so. But who is he actually – is he local?"

I could tell Mum sensed my lack of enthusiasm at the thought of her new male escort. It seemed to me so soon after Daddy's death.

Before Mum spoke, she seemed to choose her words with care.

"No, not local, love." She paused. "But he's been around the village over the winter. He worked on Mr Oliver's farm all last summer. He's always done casual farm work. He's not been called up into the army because he didn't pass his medical."

"Why not – what's wrong with him?" I asked.

"Just before the outbreak of war, he caught his left hand in a threshing machine and had to have three fingers amputated."

Mum paused to let me take this in.

I didn't know what to say about Nick. Neither of us said anything.

When Frances and Freda burst through the back door a few moments later, giggling and shoving each other playfully as usual, they were met by a somewhat embarrassed silence.

CHAPTER 11

It was a wet and windy evening. When it was windy, like it was tonight, puffs of smoke billowed down the living room chimney into the room.

They made everybody's eyes sting and water.

I volunteered to wash and undress Hugh and settle him in his cot.

I was glad to leave the smoky sitting room. When Hugh was asleep I decided to go to bed and read my library book.

During that week I found my thoughts returning

to the mysterious Nick. I wondered what sort of man he
was.

A casual farm worker didn't sound the type of
man I'd have thought Mum would permit to walk her
home, even just as a friend.

And what about the muffled giggling I'd heard on
Sunday night? Surely he could have seen her safely to
the door, without any need to actually come inside.

Mr Pickering's daughter Betty, from the Rose and
Crown, attended my school.

I decided to put out one or two feelers to find
out what information she might have on this Nick.

"Nick? Nick who?" Betty asked me. "Not the
one the blokes in the bar call 'Old Nick', like the Devil –
surely you don't mean him?"

She burst out laughing. "Not your Mum, surely?"

"I just don't know – that's why I'm asking you, you dope!"

I could feel my colour rising. I certainly didn't want my Mum to be the brunt of any public bar sniggers, whoever this Nick may be.

Betty sensed my embarrassment. She gave me a reassuring squeeze of the shoulders.

"Oh, it's nothing, Marion. You know what men are like, especially when they get a drink inside them. Nick's okay, as far as I know.

"It's just that nobody knows a great deal about him, so what they don't know they make up. You know how it is . . . "

Betty's voice trailed off and I was left wishing I'd never raised the subject with her.

But my uneasiness about his relationship with my mother remained uppermost in my mind.

CHAPTER 12

By the following Sunday my cold had almost disappeared, apart from a bit of a cough.

That night I couldn't sleep. I tossed and turned in bed, still awake close to midnight.

Then, Mum made her routine call to my bedroom. She must have sensed that I was still lying awake, despite my trying to breathe deeply as if I was sleeping.

"You awake, Marion?" Mum whispered. I could just see the outline of her head in the doorway.

"We didn't disturb you, did we? Only it's such a terrible wet night, I said Nick could sleep on the sofa downstairs rather than walk back to the farm."

Mum didn't wait for any response from me. She continued:

"I didn't want you to wonder what's happening, if he's still there when you get up tomorrow. Night, night, love. Sleep tight."

With that, she pattered off as usual to her own room and I was left to continue tossing and turning.

A little later, I began to cough in earnest. What I needed was some menthol ointment to rub on my chest. Mum kept some in her bedside cupboard.

I slipped out of bed and felt my way across to Mum's bedroom, trying not to disturb the whole house.

I grabbed the pot of ointment and quickly left

the bedroom, but not before I heard a distinctly
masculine snore.

45

Was I right to be suspicious of this man we were
sheltering under our roof?

CHAPTER 13

During the next week it became clear that Nick had moved in.

Frances and Freda cycled into the village on several evenings.

The reasons for their trips seemed quite innocent, yet I always sensed they were on a bit of a high on their return.

A great deal of whispering and giggling went on in their room, but the reason for their mirth was never mentioned at the breakfast table next day.

I really didn't like these girls, yet I couldn't exactly put my finger on the reason for my attitude.

"I bet you're a bit jealous," my friend Isabelteased, when I raised the subject with her.

"After all, they're not much older than you, are they? And you'd always been your Mum's little girl until Hugh – and then they – arrived."

I didn't really think it was that.

"They're all right," Isabel added. "Just typical townies, aren't they – you know, with their lipstick and that. Boys seem to like them, anyway. They're always hanging about with one or two boys, whenever I see them."

Yes, I told myself. Perhaps Isabel was right and that was what I felt uneasy about with the evacuees.

They're a bit older, a bit more sophisticated

and smartly dressed, and a bit more attractive to the male sex.

Just accept it, I told myself firmly. It doesn't really affect you. Yet somehow, it did.

Meanwhile, the girls stuck to their dislike of vegetables. By now, Mum was at her wits' end to know what to feed them. All they would eat was bread and jam.

Her store cupboard of last year's jam was running out and there was not enough sugar for her to make more. Frances and Freda liked sugar in their hot drinks, too.

One evening, at tea time, Nick watched Frances scrape the last traces of plum jam from the jar.

"I know!" Nick exclaimed.

"What?"

"When I was at Mr Oliver's farm he had a few bee hives in his orchard. I don't know whether he still has, but we could walk over there and see if you like," he suggested to the girls.

"Okay," they agreed. "What about tomorrow evening? There's no youth club this week, being Christmas. And it's a waste of time going to the village if there's nothing going on. Do you want to come too, Marion?" they asked me, grudgingly.

"I've got homework to do," I answered briskly, "and I said I'd help Mum put the decorations up."

As I cleared our plates from the table, I caught a sly smirk pass between the girls. No, they didn't really want me with them, I knew.

CHAPTER 14

As to Nick, I didn't go out of my way to seek his company. He was nice enough 'in small doses' – as Daddy used to remark, about anyone he didn't care for.

I wondered sometimes if Mum missed Daddy as much as I did. She seemed cheerful enough on the whole.

But I had noticed angry bruises suddenly appear on her arms lately. I didn't like that. I could think of nothing in her everyday chores which might cause them.

When her legs, too, showed signs of being held

tight, or beaten with a stick, I couldn't resist any longer

asking her the outright question.

"Well, I don't know, love. I've always been

clumsy, haven't I? Bumping into things and tripping over.

Daddy was always telling me not to rush about. To

take life more gently."

Nick came into the kitchen while we were talking.

He couldn't help but overhear the end of our

conversation. There was an uncomfortable silence.

Nick headed towards the back door. As he went

out he muttered: "Just going to the pub, Sylv. Shan't be

late."

That was the last I saw of Nick that evening,

And that was the only explanation Mum gave to

me for her bruises.

I wasn't happy at the outcome of my enquiries, but I felt I couldn't question her further.

The next evening the two evacuees and Nick left for Mr. Oliver's without even offering to help clear the dirty dishes from the table.

This was a task I'd become used to doing before they came to live with us, so I made a start while Mum got Hugh bathed in the old zinc bath in front of the sitting room fire.

There had been a gusty wind all day, with rain threatening, so, as always, smoke drifted back down the chimney. Mum made short work of Hugh's bath-time.

"I'm rubbing as much dirt back onto you as I'm taking off, my pet!" she teased him. She hauled him out and rubbed his chubby little legs briskly with the old bath towel.

Hugh smiled his cheeky grin, his small white teeth proudly displayed as he did so.

When I saw Mum relaxed and absorbed in these caring little jobs for Hugh, I forgot my concern about her bruises.

I joined in the chuckles as she slipped his almost out-grown pyjama top over his head.

He really is a big boy, and looks so much like Daddy, I thought to myself, and smiled at the memory.

CHAPTER 17

Hugh had been put to bed long ago, and I felt ready to follow him, when the back door burst open. In tumbled Frances, Freda and Nick, all in high spirits.

They were holding a jar of honey each.

"Hell's bells, Sylv, has that chimney been smoking all evening?" Nick yelled. "You can hardly see across the room!"

The girls both started coughing and made a big pantomime of fanning the smoke away with their hands.

Nick dropped into the armchair and pulled off his muddy boots.

"Who's going to offer to make a weary bloke a cup of tea, then? I suppose it's too much to hope you've got a bottle of ale hidden away somewhere?"

I moved forward to fill the kettle as Mum replied to the question of the smoky room.

"I've told you, Nick, times without number –when the wind's in the east then that chimney smokes. It needs a cap on it to stop the draught coming straight down the chimney.

"And that apple wood we're burning is damp, as well you know. It's bound to splutter, which adds to the smell!

"I can't do everything around here, much as I try," she went on.

"And it's time all you girls were in bed – it's school in the morning. I'll call you just once, remember."

Frances and Freda, still coughing, made their way towards the stairs. I warmed the old brown china tea pot, and then I followed.

"Thanks, luv, I can mash the tea,' Mum told me, with a weak smile. She passed a weary hand across her face. "You get off to bed now, too."

I left the room, with a nod to Nick. I chose to ignore the obvious ill feeling between the two adults.

I was hardly half-way up the stairs when I heard a bellow, followed by a scream and the sound of smashing pottery.

"I'll teach you to make me look small in front of them lasses," I heard Nick shout. "I've told you before – I'll see to that bloody smoking chimney when I'm good and ready.

"Now, clear up that mess and I'll have some more tea made in that little tin pot I brought with me. Even a clumsy cow like you can't break that, surely!"

I crept back and opened the door a crack – enough to see Mum's bright red, tear-stained face.

I could see that hot tea had scalded her foot and ankle. Was she upset at the pain?

Or was it because another bruise would appear in the morning, on a different part of her body?

But what could a ten-year-old do to help, either way? I pulled the staircase door shut quietly and retraced my steps to my room.

Whether the older girls had heard the rumpus I didn't know.

Next morning, nobody commented on the bandage on Mum's leg.

Only Hugh touched her bruised lip and jaw,

saying: "Poor-poor, Mumma?"

He received a hug in return.

CHAPTER 16

Every six months, Frances and Freda's mother,
Mrs Cook, came from London to see her daughters.

This was her second visit. Mum had managed, by
some miracle, to wangle a chicken from one of the
farmers who frequented the Rose and Crown.

By a further wangle Mum had got the Sunday off
work.

Mum and I didn't look forward to Mrs Cook's
visit. She never stopped talking. She spoke with a broad
Cockney accent. We found her difficult tounderstand.

And she was a chain smoker.

Still, Mum tried to make her welcome and find some news about her daughters, as we sat down to our meal.

"I hope you're not finding my girls too much to cope with, Mrs Morris," Mrs Cook said, "with two kiddies of your own to see to?"

Mrs Cook couldn't wait to light up her after-dinner fag. She offered the packet first to Mum, who refused, then to Nick, who took one. Mrs Cook lit it for him, ignoring Mum's stern glance.

"And what worries me, too," Mrs Cook went on, "is where do my girls get their money from? I've brought them two lovely winter skirts their cousin had outgrown and they practically laughed in my face!

"Said they'd just bought themselves those very items, thank you very much.

"I admit, Frances has put on so much weight, the one I'd brought for her wouldn't have been big enough, anyway. I don't know what the answer is."

"Well, considering they both live on a diet of bread and jam or honey," Mum replied, "is it any surprise they've put on weight?"

The girls scrambled from the table, hastily followed by Nick, who said he'd go and smoke outside.

This left me to clear the table and start on the inevitable washing up. Mum was unable to throw any light on Mrs Cook's questions.

There seemed to be a tension between the two women. As soon as I'd completed my task,
I offered to take Hugh a walk in his pushchair and Mum gladly accepted.

The two evacuees and Nick were lounging about

outside. I thought it strange, considering how rare Mrs

Cook's visits were.

Anyway, it was nothing to do with me.
I strapped Hugh into his buggy and tucked his little

blanket warmly around him. The wind seemed

determined to remain in the east.

Let's hope Mrs. Cook has to leave before we light

the sitting room fire, I thought to myself, or she'll

wonder what sort of conditions her daughters have to

put up with. Though I guess the smogs in London are

probably far, far worse.

It was Sunday afternoon again, and despite another windy day, I had taken Hugh out for a walk in his buggy. As we returned, it was getting dusk.

Everybody but Mum had gone out. I didn't enquire where they'd gone.

On our walk I'd picked up some tree branches to burn on the fire. I laid them on the hearth and put the kettle on for a warming drink.

Mum struggled even to get the fire to light, let alone avoid the room filling with smoke.

When Nick, Frances and Freda came in it was
the usual situation – the girls coughed and choked for
a few minutes, then went up to their bedroom.

"Want to know what I've been doing this
afternoon, Sylv?" Nick asked. Mum eyed him nervously.

Obviously a visit to the Rose and Crown had
figured in his activities, judging by his ruddy cheeks. His
hand shook as he filled his mug with tea.

"I've been round to Oliver's farm again. I've lined
up a couple of good-sized flag stones and some bricks.
I'll tackle that smoking chimney tomorrow."

Mum didn't respond.

"Well," Nick continued, "have you nothing to say
to me – like, thanks very much, Nick, how thoughtful of
you?"

He slurped his tea, leaning forward towards Mum
to press his point. She flinched slightly, then got up
and went to draw the curtains.

She moved in a wide circle around Nick, so as to
avoid being within striking distance.

I had noticed my mother flinching a lot lately,
though I'd never actually seen Nick hit her.

"Yes. Thanks," she mumbled, "let's hope the rain
holds off for you – and the wind. It's a tidy climb to the
chimney top. That's why my husband never tackled it.
Would it help if I steady the ladder while you do the
job?"

"Would it help, you ask? I'm relying on you to do
just that, woman!" Nick snapped.

Mum didn't reply.

"It won't be an easy job – not with my dodgy

hand. We won't begin too early in the day. I want to be sure I'm fully awake before I make a start. So we'll say ten o'clock, okay?"

"Right you are, Nick." Mum tried to keep it light. "That'll give me chance to do a few jobs first. Wash Hugh's nappies and such."

I wondered if Nick really would be as good as his word and do the job. I had my doubts.

Before I left for school, I reminded Mum that I was going to Isabel's house afterwards, to do some homework together.

Frances and Freda had been invited out to tea in the village, so Mum would only have Hugh and Nick to cook tea for.

CHAPTER 18

It was later than I intended before I returned home that evening. It was almost dark, but I had my cycle lamps, so the half-light was no problem.

As I pushed my bike into the shed for the night, I noticed Daddy's long wooden ladder lying across the path to the vegetable plot.

I couldn't see it very clearly but it almost seemed to be broken about two-thirds along its length.

It was too dark to see whether Nick had done the work on the chimney.

I pushed open the back door, expecting to find Mum in the kitchen clearing up from supper, as usual at this time.

But no. She and Hugh were in the sitting room. Why, I couldn't tell. It felt cold and damp in there, because no fire had been lit.

Mum was slumped in what used to be Daddy's chair. Her hair was untidy, her overall soiled. Hugh played happily with his building blocks near her feet. She seemed too weary even to acknowledge my return.

"You okay, Mum?" I queried. "Have you had any tea?"

At my question she seemed to shake herself into life and even managed a wan smile.

"I'm just tired, love. It's been a busy day, what with the work on the chimney and all. I'd love some tea.

You'll find some of those little rock cakes I made, in the red tin."

With that, she slumped back into the chair. She seemed too tired even to chat with Hugh as she generally did.

Hugh seemed to sense all was not well, too. He kicked his bricks aside, pulled himself up on Mum's skirt and climbed on to her lap.

I went to the kitchen and got our tea. It was Frances and Freda's usual choice – jam on thick slices of bread. I found the rock cakes, too.

"I bet Nick was tired, too, wasn't he, after going up and down that ladder. And carrying the flag-stones up there. It's cold in here, Mum. Must we do without a fire in this room until it's all dried out up there?"

"Yes, that's right, Marion. I'd intended to bring an oil stove in here, just to take the chill off, but then I was too tired. In any case, I remembered we're nearly out of paraffin.'

"So has Nick gone to fetch some from the shop? I didn't pass him as I came home."

I handed Mum her tea and bread and jam. As I did so, I noticed an expression I had only rarely seen on her face.

How would I describe it, I silently asked myself?

Yes, 'shifty' would be the best description I decided. Shifty, and maybe even a little guilty.

Mum leaned forward and bent over Hugh, rescuing a dribble of jam from his chin and coaxing it into his mouth.

As she raised her head I still waited for an answer, but she seemed to have forgotten I'd put the question to her. She didn't answer until I pressed the point.

"I don't know where Nick can be at present. He's probably wandered off down the pub . . ."

Her voice tailed off and she carried on drinking her tea.

Well, far be it from me to ask any more about Nick, I thought. I never had liked the man.

As far as I was concerned, I wished he would walk right back out of our lives as quickly as he had walked in.

That evening Frances and Freda came home later than they had said. They offered no explanation to Mum or myself.

I felt sure Mum was as fed up with their behaviour as I was. How much longer would these unfriendly girls be staying? 'Until the end of the war' we'd been told. That could be years yet.

Frances would be old enough to go out to work soon. Surely they'd go back to London then, and not stay around here?

But no matter how much wishful thinking I did, their stay would be as long as the powers-that-be decided.

CHAPTER 19

As the days went by, Mum became more and more quiet and withdrawn. She even seemed to have lost interest in caring for Hugh.

This was not like her. I was worried.

"You're sure you're not ill, Mum? Do you want me to have tomorrow off school to look after Hugh for you?"

"No, no, love,' she smiled half-heartedly. "It's good of you to offer, but I'll be right as rain after a good night's sleep. Lucky Hugh sleeps through

the night now. He's no trouble at all. Thanks,
anyway, love."

She patted my hand reassuringly.

A few days later, I tried again:

"Shall I take the day off school to do the chores?
It would give you a quiet day."

"No, no, Marion. You don't want to be missing
school on my account. There's nothing wrong with me."

"But there is, Mum. Can't I get you to go the
doctor's?"

But Mum wouldn't hear of it. I still felt uneasy,
but didn't know what else I could do.

The one good thing was that Nick was no longer
living at our house. I could only guess that there had
been a row between him and Mum and he had stormed
out.

I was glad to see the back of him, but I wondered if the reason Mum was so sad was because she missed him. I couldn't believe that was true. Not when I remembered those bruises.

Then suddenly the East End girls were gone.

I came back from school one day, to find Mum moping in the chair by the back door.

Hugh was playing with a toy dumper truck, filling it with gravel from the path, then emptying it again.

"Well, our wishes have been answered, Marion," Mum remarked as soon as she saw me, "though not in the way I'd have chosen."

She twisted a damp handkerchief in her lap then dabbed her eyes. She had been crying. Why?

"Our wishes?" I asked. "Which particular ones do you mean?"

We had so many wishes between us – that Daddy could have come home; that the war would end; that we had a bit more money to manage on; that we didn't need coupons to buy new clothes; that the pigeons wouldn't peck off all the raspberries before they were ripe enough to eat.

The list was endless. I couldn't see how any of these wishes couldbe granted 'not in the way I'd have chosen.'

"I had a visitor this morning,' Mum said. "Two visitors, in fact. Two ladies, each carrying official looking papers. They checked my name. Checked I had two evacuees called Frances and Freda Cook. All of which was correct, of course.

"Out of the blue, they stated they'd come to collect their belongings. Then they were off to the school to pick up the girls and drive them to the station, to catch the train back to London."

"To London?" I queried, like an idiot, "But I thought this was their home, until the war was over. Did they give a reason for this sudden change of plan?"

"The reason they gave – which I suppose I should have suspected myself – was that Frances is pregnant. She needs to be taken back nearer to her mother. She'll go to 'a home for naughty girls', as they described it. You remember Mrs Cook did comment how plump Frances had got?"

I didn't remember, but I nodded anyway.

"Mrs Cook evidently made an official complaint. She put the blame for her girl's condition on me and my 'disreputable' male lodger. I don't know where she got that word from."

Mum smiled wearily. She obviously hoped that I would accept this as sufficient explanation.

"I'd reasoned out how the girls got the money to spend on clothes," she went on. "From Nick, of course. And that's when he started to knock me about. I threatened to report him . . ."

CHAPTER 20

Before Mum could go any further, I butted in.

"So where is Nick? Does anyone know – at the pub or anywhere? Surely, if we could find him, he'd have to come clean about what he's done?"

Mum looked up from studying her work-worn hands in her lap and faced me directly. The tears welled in her eyes and she seemed oblivious to Hugh, who leaned against her knees.

"Well, you'll have to know sometime, Marion. It'll all come out soon enough, I suppose. Nick fell from the ladder that day he fixed the chimney. Didn't you guess?"

I shook my head. I didn't know what to say.

"Nick fetched two flagstones from the farm in case one wasn't enough," Mum explained. "He'd taken the first one up the ladder to the roof and come back for the second one.

"I could see he was struggling to hold the flagstone with his dodgy hand," Mum continued."The ladder was shaking a lot. And then . . .

"Well, the next thing I knew, he was hurtling down through the air, head first, towards the pond.

"He sank straight down and stayed there. You see, for some silly reason he was still hanging on to the flagstone when he fell. It was just an automatic reaction, I suppose. It must have landed on top of him, because he never came up to the surface.

"I realised there was nothing I could do."

Mum paused.

"And to be quite honest, Marion, I don't know that I'd have tried, even if there was something I could have done."

Mum let out a howl of anguish. I knelt down beside Hugh. I took one of his soft little hands in mine. With my other hand,I clasped my mother's clenched fingers.

Her head drooped as her howls of pain gradually subsided.

CHAPTER 21

"Mum?" I shook her gently. "He deserved it. And that answers the question where is Nick now. Does anybody else know?"

My distraught mother shook her head.

"Course not, Marion! I'd have kept the truth from even you if I could. But I just feel so guilty, 'cos however much I hated him – and I did –I was the one supposed to be steadying the ladder . . ."

Her voice trailed off. She rubbed her eyes again, then suddenly fell forward over Hugh and myself, onto the garden path. She just lay there. Hugh burst into noisy tears. It was a mixture of fear and surprise at Mum's unusual behaviour.

I gently lifted him up and took him into the house. I made his favourite milk shake and hastily gave him some biscuits.

I left him in the kitchen with the door slightly ajar, so that Hugh could hear my voice but not see Mum.

Mum still showed little sign of life. She was breathing but she didn't move. I rubbed her hands and spoke to her, trying to reassure her.

My mind was in turmoil. What was my best course of action? I made the decision to leave Mum where she'd fallen and walk to the nearest farm.

I'd ask to use their 'phone to contact Mr Pickering at the pub.

He'd know what to do for thebest. I also felt sure

he would keep the facts to himself, in an effort to

protect my Mum.

I fetched the pushchair, strapped Hugh in and set

off.

Somehow, we got through that day. Mum

gradually came round, and was put to bed for

a thorough rest.

Mr Pickering suggested that we explain Mum's

prolonged faint as due to her poor wartime diet and

overwork at the pub.

But, of course, Nick's disappearance had been

noticed by a lot of people. Local suspicions grew.

Everyone wanted to know the reason Nick had

vanished so suddenly.

This led toa full police investigationof the area, including our deep pond.

Mum, as the last person to have seen Nick alive, was taken into custody for further questioning.

Now it was just me and my baby brother.

CHAPTER 22

It was at this point that I realised, to the full, the support and friendship we'd received over the years from Mrs Buchan, the midwife.

As soon as it became obvious that Hugh and I were going to need to be cared for, with no adult to fend for us, Mrs Buchan stepped in. She insisted to the authorities that she was the ideal person to be our carer.

Hugh was old enough to go to nursery. I was more than capable of getting him there. I could pack a school lunch for myself, as well as dealing with laundry for us both.

We had no idea how long Mum would be kept in custody, but we managed as best we could.

A solicitor and customer at the pub, named James Firth, undertook Mum's defence, free of charge.

"After all, we were all aware Nick was a bad lot and Sylvia as innocent as the day is fair," he announced publicly. "She'd just been pushed too far, too often, poor woman."

Although things fell into place so well at Mrs Buchan's, I still felt drawn to return to our real home. Mrs Buchan insisted that I limit my visits home to weekends.

One particular Saturday, I decided to go home on my bike to check all was well. I would pick up any post, then cycle straight back.

I took a small can of oil with me. Lately, the large back door key had been difficult to turn. But there was no need for me to struggle, as the door was just slightly ajar.

That made me very uneasy. My heart was thumping as I pushed the door further open.

To my relief, there was nobody in the kitchen. I crept forward,holding my breath, I went and peeped into the cold, gloomy sitting room. There was a shabby figure seated in what had always been Daddy's chair.

I shrank back as the stranger turned towards the door. To my amazement I heard it whisper: "Marion?"

Then I knew that this was no stranger. It was Daddy! I stumbled headlong into my father's arms.

Laughing and crying at the same time, we were both lost in the wonder of the moment.

CHAPTER 23

Looking back now,over those six years, this is the memory which remains most vividly in my mind.

What a brilliant surprise it was to realise my father was alive. And what a bonus it was, after the recent weeks of stress and tension.

"But how can it be you?" I stammered. "We had an official letter saying you were dead!"

"Well, you don't want to believe all you read in official letters, my girl," Daddy reassured me.

"So what happened to you?"

"I was taken prisoner," Daddy explained, "but as my captors took me along a riverside path, I was able to escape. I found a hiding place in undergrowth on the river bank until it was dark.

"Then, I started to travel cross-country. I sheltered in farm buildings, found scraps of food growing in the fields and eventually I reached the coast. It took months to gradually make my way back to England.

"Now," he continued, "what about your mother? I thought I must be mistaken when I saw her photo in a newspaper. But it was her, right enough – poor lass! She must be desperate."

All I wanted was for Daddy to come back with me to the village.

But despite all my attempts to persuade him, he wouldn't. He insisted on staying in our old house.

Of course, I wanted to stay with him but he said no, I couldn't do that.

So after a tearful goodbye, I cycled back to Mrs Buchan's in a turmoil of joy and despair – first one emotion, then the other.

I never said a word about my wonderful news until Little Hugh was settled into bed with a specially warm kiss from me, followed by one from Mrs Buchan.

Back in the sitting room, Mrs Buchan turnedto me:

"Come on, Marion – spit it out! I can tell you've something to tell me."

I stammered out my news as quickly as I could.

"Hang on, hang on, Marion. Are you telling me your Dad's alive?"

I nodded.

"That's impossible – what about the official letter?"

With a smile, I repeated my father's reply to my identical question.

"You can't believe all you read in official letters, Mrs Buchan!"

"Even so, dear, I think you should be wary of telling people the news," she warned. "Your Dad will have to be careful that he's not charged with deserting from the army. I've never come across a situation like this before.

"I think we should keep it our secret for now. I know it will be difficult for you, but you don't want to get your family into yet more trouble, do you?"

She patted my hand gently, seeing the disappointment in my face. I wouldn't be able to tell even my best friend, Isabel.

Or even Mum, when I next visited her.

It was going to be very hard.

CHAPTER 24

The problem soon resolved itself, however.
Daddy thought he hadn't been noticed as he returned
across the fields from the station to our house.

But pigeon pie was a very popular dish at the
Rose and Crown. The landlord, Mr Pickering, had been in
the trees behind our house, shooting pigeons, as Daddy
returned home.

Despite Daddy's shabby appearance, the pub
landlord recognised him. After closing time that Sunday
afternoon, he returned to our house.

Bert Pickering was normally a jovial man. However, when Daddy answered his knock on the door, he became very emotional at the sight of his old school pal.The two men could do nothing but hug each other, wordlessly.

Then questions and answers flew between them. It was almost an hour later before they tried to formulate some plan of action.

"We've already got up a petition in the village on behalf of your Sylv," Bert announced. "And there's something else that should carry some weight.

"That young scamp Frances, one of the evacuees, read about Sylv's case in the papers.She has written to say that Nick was the father ofher baby. He forced himself on her without herconsent! Now, what do you think of that, eh?"

Daddy had to be brought up to date. He didn't

know who Frances or Nick were. In fact, nobody was very clear who Nick was, actually – just that he was a casual farm labourer and trouble maker.

None of us witnessed Daddy's first visit to Mum in prison, but we could all imagine what a joyous occasion it was.

Mr Firth, the solicitor, was a star. He spoke most movingly on Mum's behalf. He pressed the point that there were extreme extenuating circumstances.

It was a relief when – due to Mum being the only person to witness Nick's fall from the ladder – a verdict of accidental death was brought.

Our jubilant family returned home that day with Mum and Daddy arm in arm and Little Hugh riding confidently on Big Hugh's shoulders. We all felt it was a perfect ending to a very long, troubled period.

CHAPTER 25

We had reckoned without a visitor that evening. Mum was just drawing the curtains, with a sigh of relief that we were all safely back.

Relief, too, that the freshly lit sitting room fire was burning brightly, with not a sign of any smoking chimney. It was the first fire since the capping stone was put in position.

There was a sharp knock on the back door – followed by Mr Pickering's cheery face peering into the sitting room.

"I reckon I know you all well enough now to walk straight in – right?" he chuckled.

Daddy rushed to give him a bear hug and Little Hugh flung his arms round Bert's knees. Mum and I stood back,mopping our eyes with screwed-up, soggy hankies.

"I have a proposition to make to you, Hugh and Sylv. I want you to hear me out and take time about making a decision, if you wish.

"I know you and I were at school together, Hugh, and a fine figure of a man you still are, despite all your difficulties.

"You may know that the reason I wasn't called up into the army at the same time as you, at the beginning of the war, is that I had a spot of heart trouble.

"Nothing major.Nothing a pub landlord can't cope with, you understand?

"But, as so often happens, the condition of the old ticker has worsened over that period and I've decided to take early retirement.

"I've managed to save a bit, and – something else you may not be aware of – I've been courting Mrs Buchan, the midwife, for a number of years.

"She, too, feels she's too old to be running round the countryside helping bring these little monsters into the world." He ruffled Little Hugh's hair affectionately.

"So, as you can see, everything's fallen into place nicely. Mrs Buchan is quite content for me to share her cottage . . ."

He looked around, judging the right moment for his final announcement. We were all wondering what all these happy snippets of news had to do with our family.

"I couldn't have employed a better barmaid than you, Sylv," he concluded.

"And you, Hugh,you'll be looking round for work, I assume? So how about you taking on as landlord and lady of the Rose and Crown?

"You'd be very popular with the regulars, I know. And there's quite a decent bit of garden at the back for Little Hugh to play in. What do you say?"

"I say let's drink to that, Bert,"Daddy exclaimed. He turned to my mum.

"So what do you say, love? You're the one with all the experience – I've never stepped that side of the bar in my life!"

Mum didn't have to reply in words. She just left the room, and returned almost immediately with glasses and a small bottle of dark,purple,syrupy liquid. She handed it to Daddy.

"Home-made sloe gin. Bert, I'm sure we'd both be delighted to take up your very generous offer."

Daddy turned to Mum with a wide grin on his face, which she instantly returned.

Then she placed her hands on either side of Bert Pickering's red face and surprised him with a smacking kiss of thanks.

CHAPTER 26

I was brought back to the present by Mum bustling into the kitchen, obviously hoping to clear the breakfast table and wash up before opening time.

"Marion! You've nowhere near finished opening your cards and presents! Here, let me warm that chocolate up for you – it won't be worth drinking now it's cold."

Then she saw that in my hand I still held Isabel's birthday card.

"You've been daydreaming, haven't you, my girl?" she continued.

"I suppose so," I admitted.

Those past childhood memories I'd been reliving seemed so vivid still.

"Thanks, Mum. I'll wash these pots as soon as I've drunk my chocolate. I know Saturday lunchtimes are always busy."

Mum squeezed my shoulders appreciatively.

"You are a pet, Marion. I don't know what I'd have done without you."

And we both knew she wasn't just referring to the washing up.